ABUELITA

¿QUÉ VAMOS HACER HOY?
LET'S MAKE
ROSCA DE REYES!

BILINGUAL VERSION

WRITTEN BY MILLIE FLORES

ILLUSTRATED BY CLAUDIA GUZES

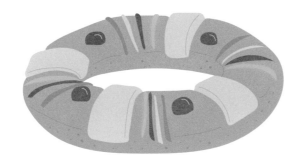

Todos los sábados mi Mamí takes me to stay with mi Abuelita while she goes to work. This morning she's running a little late, so we are hurrying to grandma's.

"¡Amá! ¡Ya llegamos!" calls my mom when we let ourselves into Abuelita's house.

Mi Abuelita comes to the door from the kitchen with a bag in her hand.

"Buenos días María. Buenos días Lupita. Ten, mija. I made you a torta for lunch." She hands my mom the bag.

"Gracias Amá. I have to get going. I'll be late!" says my mom.

"Qué tengas un buen día, mija." responds Abuelita as my mom rushes out the door with her lunch.

"¡Abuelita! ¿Qué vamos a hacer hoy?"

"¡Ah! Today's a special day! We are going to make the Rosca de Reyes cake for El Día de Los Reyes Magos!"

"I can't wait! Do you think Los Reyes will bring me something, Abuelita?"

"Pues, I can't say. Have you been a good girl this year?"

"¡Sí!"

"Well then, I expect they will. Now, let's see what we need to make our cake."

Abuelita opens the fridge and checks some containers on the counter.
"Hmm, it looks like I'm out of eggs. We also need oranges, some figs, cherries, dulce de acitrón, and some quince stripes. Let's go to the mercado and get those!"

I love going to the mercado. There is so much to see and do. We head right to Doña Elena's vegetable stand to buy what we need.

"Buenos días Doña Lupe. Buenos días Lupita. ¿Qué van a hacer hoy?"

"Buenos días Doña Elena. We're going to make the Rosca de Reyes cake!"

"¡Excelente Lupita! ¿Te portaste bien este año? ¿Los Reyes van a traerte algo, verdad?"

"¡Sí!"

"¡Qué bien! Now, Doña Lupe, what can I get for you this morning?"

"I need una docena de blanquillos, tres naranjas, dulce de acitrón, un poco de ate de membrillo, dos higos, and unas cerezas. Oh, and a cup of azúcar glas."

Doña Elena weighs our purchases and hands them over to us, smiling.

"¡Gracias Elena!"

"Gracias, Doña Lupe. Adiós Lupita."

Abuelita puts the fruit and sugar into her bag. She hands me the bag of eggs to carry. I have to remember not to swing my arms on the way home, so I don't break any.

We head home and lay the ingredients out on the table in the kitchen.

"¿Qué vamos a hacer primero, Abuelita?"

"First, we need to heat the water a little bit. Can you fill this pot for me?"

"¡Claro que sí, Abuelita!"

I take the small pot over to the garrafón and add water. It's heavy when I finish, and I spill a little on the floor.

"No te preocupes, Lupita. Use the mop and dry the floor, so we don't slip and fall."

"Ok, Abuelita." I get the mop from the patio and clean up the mess I made. Meanwhile, Abuelita turns on the stove to heat the water and gathers the other ingredients.

As soon as the water is warm, Abuelita pours it into a mixing bowl and adds a packet of yeast. She gives me a fork and tells me to mix it. Then we set it aside to get foamy.

In another bowl, Abuelita puts the flour, eggs, sugar, salt, milk, and melted butter. She hands me the grater and tells me to grate the orange peel, so I do.

When the yeast mixture bubbles up, Abuelita adds some flour and covers the bowl with a towel. Then she kneads the mixture in the bigger bowl until it's crumbly. She lets me try, but my arms get tired.

Whew! This is a lot of work! Abuelita adds the yeast mixture to the flour mixture. I dust some flour on the table so the masa won't get stuck, and then she starts to throw it around and punch it.

She lets me try that, and it's so much fun! When she finishes, the ball of dough is shiny and soft. She puts it in a big bowl and covers it with a towel again.

Abuelita melts some butter on the stove. She adds the azúcar glas. It's slippery, not like regular sugar. And then she puts in some flour and the egg yolk. She stirs and stirs until everything is creamy.

When I check on the ball of dough, I see it's bigger now! It's like a living creature!

I put some more flour on the table, and Abuelita rolls and punches it some more. She rolls the dough into a long worm and then connects the two ends into an oval.

She puts this on a baking sheet and covers it with a towel. While we wait for it to rise, Abuelita tells me about why we have Rosca de Reyes on January 7.

Rosca is a special type of bread, and Reyes are kings. The Kings' bread is a circle or oval shape like a crown and covered in candied fruit like jewels. Inside is el Niño Dios, a plastic baby Jesús. It's hidden inside because baby Jesús had to be hidden from the bad King Herod's soldiers who were trying to kill him.

It's time to decorate it with the fruits and hide the baby Jesús inside. Abuelita lets me put on all the fruit after she brushes the top with an egg mixture.

First, I put on the stripes of red and green quince that she slices for me from the blocks of ate de membrillo.

Then I add some candied acitrón. Those are my favorite! I add just a few higos because they aren't very tasty and five cherries.

Finally, I put on a few pieces of almonds.

Then Abuelita pushes the baby inside the dough and slides the rosca into the oven to cook.

As the rosca bakes, Abuelita talks more about Los Reyes Magos.

These wise men followed a star and traveled for many days to visit the baby Jesús and his parents, María and José.

Their names were Melchor, Gaspar, and Baltasar, and they brought very expensive gifts, el oro, el incienso, y la mirra.

They were warned in a dream not to return to tell King Herod where the Holy family was and went home by another route.

José took his wife María and the baby Jesús and ran away to Egypt.

"Have you written your letter to Los Reyes Magos, Lupita?" asks Abuelita.

"Not yet. Will you help me?"

"Sí, mi vida. There's some paper and a pencil on the table next to my bed. Go and get it, and we'll write it ahorita." I rush into Abuelita's room and grab the tablet and pencil and rush back out to the kitchen.

"First, we need to write the date and greeting. I'll write it on this piece of paper, and you can copy it on yours." says Abuelita.

I'm not very good at writing my letters yet. I make a mistake and have to start again on a clean piece of paper.

"Now, have you been a good girl Lupita?" asks Abuelita.

"¡Sí!" I say.

"Then let's tell Los Reyes that. Write 'Me he portado bien durante todo el año. Ayudo a mi Mamí en casa y mi Abuelita cuando cocina.'

"Next, let's tell Los Reyes what you would like this year."

"Hmm. Well, I want a molcajete like yours, Abuelita. And a table and chairs for my muñecas."

"You can choose one more, Lupita. Remember, each Rey will bring you one gift."

Sábado, 6 de enero

Queridos Reyes Magos

Me he portado bien durante todo
el año. Ayudo a mi mami en casa
y a mi abuelita cuando cocina.
Este año quiero un molcajete como
el que tiene mi abuelita, un
juego de té de barro y una mesa
con sillas para mis muñecas.

¡Que tengan buenas noches!
Con mucho cariño,
Maria Guadalupe (Lupita)

"Hmm. Maybe un juego de té de barro for my muñecas too."

"Those sound like excellent gifts. Let's write them down in the letter. Finally, you should sign your name."

"Will Los Reyes know it is me if I sign María Guadalupe?"

"You can write 'Lupita' after that so that they know for sure if you like. Now you can draw some pictures on the letter. There are some colored pencils in the box on the shelf over there."

I set to work drawing some stars and a picture of the table and chairs I want, and I try to draw some camellos, but they don't look much like camels. I fold the letter in half, and on the outside, I write: A Sus Majestades Los Reyes Magos de Oriente so that they will know the letter is for them.

Tonight I am going to spend the night with Abuelita, so I need to collect some grass for los animales that Los Reyes Magos ride to leave with my letter and my shoes. I go out to Abuelita's garden.

In the very back, I find some garbanzo and a tiny patch of alfalfa. Those will be perfect! I take the scissors off the nail by the back door and carefully snip a handful of each. Then I put the scissors back on the nail and show Abuelita what I found.

"¡Excelente Lupita! Those animals will have a feast, and Los Reyes Magos will be happy and might just bring you everything you asked for!"

"Oh, I hope so, Abuelita!"

I put my shoes at the end of my bed before I go to sleep, next to the food and my letter to Los Reyes Magos.

I am sure I'll never get to sleep. I am so excited!

Before I know it, it's morning, and Abuelita comes in to wake me up.

"Lupita, did you hear the noise los animales made last night? They were chuffing, and their hooves clacked on the tile so loudly they woke me up! I came in to see what was happening, and there they were! They were so big I couldn't believe they fit into this tiny room!"

"What happened Abuelita?"

"Well, I shushed them and told Los Reyes that they'd better be quiet, or they'd wake you. They said the animals were so happy to have some garbanzo and alfalfa that they were dancing, and that's why there was so much noise."

"I knew they'd like it!" I clap my hands happily.

"They did! Then one of the Reyes asked me if you had been a good girl."

"What did you tell them, Abuelita?" I worry maybe they didn't leave anything for me after all.

"I said that you had been. You help your Mamí every day, and you help me when you visit."

"Did they leave me anything, Abuelita? Did they?"

I can hardly stand it.

"Hmm, yes, I believe they did. Down there at the end of your bed. Go ahead and take a look." she says, smiling.

I scramble from under the covers and nearly fall out of bed in my excitement. All the alfalfa and garbanzo are gone!

My letter is gone too!

But in their places, there is a little molcajete and pink table and chairs for my dolls.

There is also a tea set!! It's perfect for my dolls and me to have afternoon tea later!

A little later in the morning, my Mamí arrives with her síster, my Tía Rosa, and her husband, Pedro. They bring some atole, so I know it's time to cut the cake.

Each person cuts their own piece, as big or small as they want, and puts it on their plate. Everyone gets a cherry. I am extra careful with the knife because it's so sharp!

Abuelita serves everyone a cup of atole, and we start to eat. I poke my piece looking for el Niño Dios but don't see it.

Suddenly, Abuelita makes a noise and pulls something from her mouth. It's the baby Jesús! The person who gets it is in charge of making tamales for el Día de la Candelaria on February 2.

Abuelita says "Lupita, tráeme mi bolsa."

I run to the other room and bring back Abuelita's purse. She opens it, takes out her change purse, and slips the little baby in with her coins.

"Para la suerte." she says.

We finish our cake and atole and clean the kitchen up for Abuelita. Then it's time to go.

"Abuelita, can I help you make the tamales? Can I? I have a molcajete now."
I ask.

"Claro que sí, Lupita. I couldn't make them without you. In fact, we'll have a tamalada, and your Mamí and Tía Rosa can come and help too. Would you like that?"

"¡Sí!" I scream.

I can't wait for the tamalada!

40

CAN YOU HELP LUPITA GATHER THESE INGREDIENTS?

MILK
EGGS
ORANGES
CHERRIES
A STICK OF BUTTER
CINNAMON STICKS
ATE DE MEMBRILLO VERDE

42

ROSCA DE REYES RECIPE

INGREDIENTS

- 1/4 CUP WARM WATER (105°F TO 115°F)
- 1 ENVELOPE OF DRY ACTIVE YEAST
- 4 1/2 CUPS FLOUR
- 1/3 CUP WARM MILK (105°F TO 115°F)
- 3/4 CUP OF SUGAR
- 6 EGGS
- 1/2 TEASPOON SALT
- 1 1/4 TEASPOONS GROUND CINNAMON
- 1 1/2 TABLESPOON ORANGE OR VANILLA EXTRACT
- 2 STICKS OF BUTTER, SOFTENED
- FRESHLY GRATED ORANGE ZEST FROM 1 1/2 LARGE ORANGES
- 1/2 CUP CONFECTIONERS' SUGAR
- CANDIED DRIED FRUIT LIKE FIGS, CANDIED ACITRÓN (ECHINOCACTUS PLATYACANTHUS), RED AND GREEN QUINCE PASTE STRIPES (ATE DE MEMBRILLO), OR CHERRIES AND SLICED ALMONDS

ADD THE YEAST TO THE WARM WATER IN A SMALL BOWL.

STIR IN 1 TABLESPOON OF GRANULATED SUGAR. ALLOW IT TO SIT UNTIL IT BUBBLES UP.

ADD 3/4 CUP OF SOFTENED BUTTER TO THE WARM MILK IN ANOTHER BOWL AND STIR.

MIX 2 CUPS OF FLOUR, 1/3 CUP OF GRANULATED SUGAR, 4 EGGS, 1 TEASPOON OF CINNAMON, AND THE SALT INTO A LARGE BOWL UNTIL WELL-BLENDED.

ADD THE YEAST MIXTURE, BUTTER AND MILK MIXTURE, AND THE VANILLA OR ORANGE EXTRACT AND MIX AGAIN.

GRADUALLY ADD 2 CUPS OF FLOUR. THE DOUGH WILL BE SLIGHTLY STICKY.

DUST A FLAT SURFACE WITH FLOUR.

KNEAD THE DOUGH FOR ABOUT 15 MINUTES UNTIL IT IS SMOOTH.

PUT THE KNEADED DOUGH IN A BUTTERED BOWL.

FLIP THE DOUGH SO THAT THE BUTTERED SIDE IS UP.

COVER THE BOWL WITH A TOWEL AND ALLOW IT TO RISE FOR 1 TO 2 HOURS UNTIL IT DOUBLES IN SIZE.

MIX 1/4 CUP OF BUTTER AND CONFECTIONERS' SUGAR UNTIL BLENDED.

ADD 1/2 CUP FLOUR AND 1/4 TEASPOON CINNAMON, AND THE YOLK FROM ONE EGG.

BLEND UNTIL IT BECOMES A SMOOTH PASTE.

DIVIDE IT INTO EQUAL PIECES AND WRAP IT IN PLASTIC WRAP. SET ASIDE.

ONCE THE DOUGH HAS RISEN, PUNCH IT DOWN. KNEAD ON A FLOURED SURFACE AND SHAPE INTO A BALL.

ROLL THE BALL INTO A 2-INCH LOG.

PLACE IT ON A BAKING SHEET, BRINGING THE ENDS TOGETHER TO FORM AN OVAL.

COVER WITH A KITCHEN TOWEL AND LET IT RISE UNTIL IT DOUBLES IN SIZE.

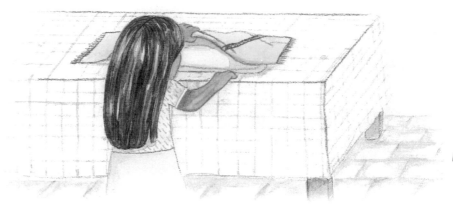

PREHEAT THE OVEN TO 350°F.

WHISK 1 EGG AND A LITTLE MILK TOGETHER UNTIL WELL BLENDED.

BRUSH THE DOUGH RING WITH THE EGG MIXTURE.

ROLL THE PIECES OF CONFECTIONERS' SUGAR MIXTURE INTO STRIPS AND ARRANGE THEM AS YOU LIKE ON THE DOUGH RING.

PRESS CANDIED DRIED FRUIT LIKE FIGS, CANDIED ACITRÓN, RED AND GREEN QUINCE PASTE STRIPES (ATE DE MEMBRILLO), OR CHERRIES AND SLICED ALMONDS ALONG THE DOUGH RING AS YOU LIKE.

INSERT THE PLASTIC FIGURE FROM THE BOTTOM, MAKING SURE IT DOES NOT TOUCH THE BAKING SHEET.

BAKE FOR ABOUT 30 MINUTES UNTIL GOLDEN BROWN. THE DOUGH WILL SOUND HOLLOW WHEN TAPPED.

NOTE:

DULCE DE ACITRÓN IS A TRADITIONAL SWEET MADE FROM THE CENTER OF THE GIANT BARREL CACTUS (ECHINOCACTUS PLATYACANTHUS). THESE CACTI CAN LIVE FOR MORE THAN A HUNDRED YEARS.

IN RECENT YEARS, IT HAS BECOME AN ENDANGERED SPECIES. BECAUSE IT GROWS SO SLOWLY, ANY PART OF THIS PLANT SHOULD BE HARVESTED SUSTAINABLY.

GLOSSARY

IN ORDER OF APPEARANCE IN THE STORY

- ABUELITA (AH-BWAY-LEE-TAH) GRANDMA

- ¿QUÉ VAMOS A HACER HOY? (KEH BAH-MOHS AH AH-SEHR OH-EE) WHAT ARE WE GOING TO DO TODAY?

- ROSCA DE REYES (ROHS-KAH DEH REH-YEHS) KING'S CAKE, A TRADITIONAL CAKE EATEN IN MEXICO ON JANUARY 6TH TO CELEBRATE THE EPIPHANY

- TODOS LOS SÁBADOS (TOH-DOHS LOHS SAH-BAH-THOHS) EVERY SATURDAY

- MI MAMÍ (MEE MAH-MEE) MY MOMMY

- ¡AMÁ! (AH-MAH) MOM!

- ¡YA LLEGAMOS! (YAH YEH-GAH-MOHS) WE'VE ARRIVED!

- BUENOS DÍAS (BWAY-NOHS DEE-AHS) GOOD MORNING

- TEN (TEN) HERE, HAVE THIS.

- MIJA (MEE-HAH) MY DAUGHTER

- TORTA (TORE-TAH) A TYPE OF SANDWICH POPULAR IN LATIN AMERICA

- GRACIAS (GRAH-SEE-YAHS) THANK YOU

- ¡QUÉ TENGAS UN BUEN DÍA! (KEH TEHN-GAHS OON BWEHN DEE-AH) HAVE A GOOD DAY!

- EL DÍA DE LOS REYES MAGOS (EHL DEE-AH DEH LOHS REH-YEHS MAH-GOHS) THREE KINGS' DAY, A HOLIDAY CELEBRATED IN SPAIN AND LATIN AMERICA ON JANUARY 6TH TO COMMEMORATE THE ARRIVAL OF THE MAGI TO VISIT THE BABY JESUS

- PUES (PWEHS) WELL... (A FILLER WORD USED TO EXPRESS AGREEMENT OR TO START A SENTENCE)

- ¡SÍ! (SEE) YES!

- DULCE DE ACITRÓN (DOOL-SEH DEH AH-THEE-TROHN) CANDIED CITRON, A TYPE OF CANDY MADE FROM THE FRUIT OF THE BIZNAGA CACTUS

- MERCADO (MEHR-KAH-DOH) MARKET

- DOÑA (DOHN-YAH) AN HONORIFIC TITLE USED BEFORE A WOMAN'S NAME, SIMILAR TO "MADAME"

- ¿QUÉ VAN A HACER HOY? (KEH BAHN AH AH-SEHR OH-EE) WHAT ARE YOUR GOING TO DO TODAY?

- ¡EXCELENTE! (EKS-EH-LEHN-TEH) EXCELLENT!

- ¿TE PORTASTE BIEN ESTE AÑO? (TEH POHR-TAH-STEH BYEHN EHS-TEH AH-NYOH) DID YOU BEHAVE WELL THIS YEAR?4

- ¿LOS REYES VAN A TRAERTE ALGO, VERDAD? (LOHS REH-YEHS BAHN AH TRAH-EHR-TEH AHL-GOH BEHR-THAHD) THE THREE KINGS ARE GOING TO BRING YOU SOMETHING, RIGHT?

- ¡QUÉ BIEN! (KEH BYEHN) HOW GREAT!

- UNA DOCENA DE BLANQUILLOS (OO-NAH DOH-SEH-NAH DEH BLAHN-KEE-HOHS) A DOZEN EGGS

- TRES NARANJAS (TREHS NAH-RAHN-HAHS) THREE ORANGES

- UN POCO DE ATE DE MEMBRILLO (OON POH-KOH DEH AH-TEH DEH MEM-BREE-HOH) A LITTLE BIT OF QUINCE PASTE, A SWEET SPREAD MADE FROM THE FRUIT OF THE QUINCE TREE

- DOS HIGOS (DOHS EE-GOHS) TWO FIGS

- UNAS CEREZAS (OO-NAHS THEH-REH-THAHS) SOME CHERRIES

- AZÚCAR GLAS (AH-THOO-KAHR GLAHS) POWDERED SUGAR

- ADIÓS (AH-DYOHS) GOODBYE

- PRIMERO (PREE-MEH-ROH) FIRST

- ¡CLARO QUE SÍ! (KLAH-ROH KEH SEE) OF COURSE!

- GARRAFÓN (GAH-RAH-FON) LARGE WATER JUG

- ¡NO TE PREOCUPES! (NOH TEH PREH-OH-KOO-PEHS) DON'T WORRY!

- MASA (MAH-SAH) CORN DOUGH

- EL NIÑO DIOS (EL NEEN-YOH THOHS) THE CHRIST CHILD

- MARÍA (MAH-REE-AH) MARY

- JOSÉ (HOH-SEH) JOSEPH

- JESÚS (HEH-SOOS) JESUS

- MELCHOR, GASPAR, AND BALTASAR (MEHL-KOHR GAHS-PAHR GAHL-VAH-SAHR) MELCHIOR, CASPER, AND BALTHAZAR (THE THREE WISE MEN OR MAGI WHO VISITED JESUS AFTER HIS BIRTH)

- EL ORO, EL INCIENSO, Y LA MIRRA (EL OH-ROH EL EEN-THEE-EHN-SOH EE LAH MEER-RAH) GOLD, FRANKINCENSE, AND MYRRH

- MI VIDA (MEE VEE-DAH) MY LIFE

- AHORITA (AH-OH-REE-TAH) RIGHT NOW

- ME HE PORTADO BIEN DURANTE TODO EL AÑO. (MEH EH POHR-TAH-DOH BYEHN DOOR-AHN-TEH TOH-DOH EL AHN-YOH) I HAVE BEHAVED WELL THROUGHOUT THE YEAR.

- AYUDO A MI MAMÍ EN CASA Y MI ABUELITA CUANDO COCINA. (AH-YOO-DOH AH MEE MAH-MEE EHN KAH-SAH EE MEE AH-BWEH-LEE-TAH KWAHN-DOH KOH-SEE-NAH) I HELP MY MOM AT HOME AND MY GRANDMA WHEN SHE COOKS.

- MOLCAJETE (MOHL-KAH-HEH-TEH) MORTAR AND PESTLE, A TRADITIONAL MEXICAN COOKING TOOL

- MUÑECAS (MOO-NYEH-KAHS) DOLLS

- UN JUEGO DE TÉ DE BARRO (OON HWEH-GOH DEH TEH DEH BAH-ROH) A SET OF CLAY TEACUPS

- CAMELLOS (KAH-MEH-LOHS) CAMELS

- A SUS MAJESTADES LOS REYES MAGOS DE ORIENTE (AH SOOS MAH-CHES-TAH-DEHS LOHS REH-YEHS MAH-GOHS DEH OH-REE-EHN-TEH) TO THEIR MAJESTIES THE THREE WISE MEN FROM THE EAST, A COMMON GREETING IN LETTERS TO THE THREE WISE MEN

- LOS ANIMALES (LOHS AH-NEE-MAH-LEHS) THE ANIMALS

- GARBANZO (GAHR-BAHN-THOH) CHICKPEA

- TÍA (TEE-AH) AUNT

- ATOLE (AH-TOH-LEH) A TRADITIONAL MEXICAN HOT BEVERAGE MADE WITH CORN DOUGH, WATER, AND SWEETENERS LIKE SUGAR AND CINNAMON

- TAMALES (TAH-MAH-LEHS) A TRADITIONAL MEXICAN DISH MADE OF MASA FILLED WITH VARIOUS INGREDIENTS AND STEAMED IN CORN HUSKS

- EL DÍA DE LA CANDELARIA (EL DEE-AH DEH LAH KAHN-DEH-LAH-REE-AH) CANDLEMAS DAY

- TRÁEME MI BOLSA. /TRAH-EH-MEH MEE BOHL-SAH/ BRING ME MY BAG.

- PARA LA SUERTE /PAH-RAH LAH SWER-TEH/ FOR LUCK

- TAMALADA /TAH-MAH-LAH-DAH/ REFERS TO A SOCIAL GATHERING WHERE TAMALES ARE MADE AND EATEN

Made in the USA
Columbia, SC
26 November 2024

47581178R10033